Wolf

WATCH

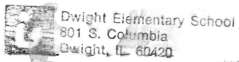

Wolf
WATCH

BY Kay Winters

ILLUSTRATED BY

Laura Regan

SIMON & SCHUSTER BOOKS FOR YOUNG READERS

SIMON & SCHUSTER BOOKS FOR YOUNG READERS
An imprint of Simon & Schuster Children's Publishing Division
1230 Avenue of the Americas, New York, New York 10020

Book design by Paul Zakris
The text for this book is set in 22-point Centaur Bold
The illustrations are rendered in oil paint
Printed and bound in the United States of America
First Edition
10 9 8 7 6 5 4 3 2 1

LIBRARY OF CONGRESS CATALOGING-IN-PUBLICATION DATA
Winters, Kay.
Wolf watch / written by Kay Winters ; illustrated by Laura Regan.
p. cm.
Summary: After spending their first few weeks being cared for in the safety of
their den, four wolf pups emerge to face a world full of wonder and danger.
ISBN 0-689-80218-8
1. Wolves—Juvenile fiction. 2. Wolves—Fiction.
3. Animals—Infancy—Fiction. I. Regan, Laura, ill. II. Title.
PZ10.3.W6885Wo 1997
[E] dc20 95-19628

Reprinted by arrangement with Simon & Schuster Books for Young Readers.

Acknowledgments

Special thanks for answering my questions about wolves to:
Barbara Benson, Associate Professor in Biology, Cedar Crest College,
Allentown, Pennsylvania; and L. David Mech, Wildlife Research
Biologist, National Biological Service, University of Minnesota.

Appreciation to my editor, Stephanie Owens Lurie,
who knows the importance of encouragement.
—K. W.

Wolf Watch *is dedicated to my husband,*
Earl D. Winters, for his love and support
—K. W.

Dedicated with love and thanks to Mom and Dad
for teaching me to stand on my own
—L. R.

High on the hill
On a velvet night,
While the moon is rising
Seven wolves watch.

Down in the den
Where the dark is deep,
Pups in her belly,
Mother Wolf waits.

High on the hill
In a tall pine tree,
Hidden in branches
An eagle stirs.

Down in the den
Deep in the dark,
One–two–three–four
Pups are born.

High on the hill
Seven gray wolves
Sing out with joy
While the eagle dreams.

Down in the den
Close to their mother,
Eyes shut tight,
Pups suckle and sleep.

Riding on wind
Eagle, wings wide,
Circles the hillside
Eyeing the pack.

Off to the forest,
Father Wolf sniffs.
Wolves weave like shadows,
Stalking a deer.

Deep in the den
Mother washes the pups.
Their eyes open blue.
Soon their ears start to perk.

Home from a hunt,
Meat for the mother.
Father Wolf listens,
Pups whimper and growl.

Deep in the den
Pups teeter and totter.
They tumble and stumble
On short stubby legs.

In the tall tree
Eagle watches wolves go.
He sails by the den's hole.
His shadow comes close.

Mother Wolf pushes
The pups toward the tunnel.
Time to come out,
Meet the rest of the pack.

Out of the darkness
Into the light.
Four furry wolf pups
Blink at their world.

In the tall pine
The eagle is watching.
He has been waiting
For little wolf pups.

Bird songs and spring leaves.
Blue sky and soft sun.
Gray wolves with tail wags
Welcome the pups.

Sniffing the sweet smells,
Pups taste the sunshine.
Meet brothers and sisters,
Are kissed with a lick.

One pup wanders off.
She follows a cricket.
She waits—then she pounces.
But the cricket leaps free.

WATCH OUT! EAGLE!
Dives straight at the pup!
Little Wolf looks up
As the bird rockets down.

Pup stumbles sideways
And sinks to the ground.
Eyes wide, ears back,
She makes herself small.

Her heartbeat is bursting.
Eagle stretches his legs.
He's almost upon her.
His talons brush fur.

With a sizzling snarl
Father leaps to Pup's side.
He lunges at feathers.
Eagle lifts off—alone.

Missed—by a moment.
The bird screams in rage.
With Father beside her
Little Pup scurries home.

Down in the den
Four pups are sleeping,
One on the other,
With Mother nearby.

High on the hill
Seven gray wolves
Lift up their voices
And sing to the sky.